Written and Created by
Tom Hutchison

Pencils: Ian Snyder

Inks: Sony Merbitt and Troy Zurel

Colors: Luis Guerrero and Ceci de la Cruz

Lettered by HDE

Cover Artists
Natali Sanders
Eric Basaldua, Corey Knaebel
Sebastian Cichon, Jenevieve Broomall
Jesse Wichmann, Nei Ruffino

Design: Rob Duenas and Jesse Wichmann

URSA MINOR VOL 1. August 2013. Published by Big Dog Ink. Office of publication: 2301 Wing Street Rolling Meadows, IL 6008. Copyright © 2013 Tom Hutchison. All rights reserved. URSA MINOR (including all prominent characters featured herin), it's logo and all character likenesses are trademarks of Tom Hutchison unless otherwise noted. No part of this publication may be reproduced or transmitted, in any form or by any means (except for short exerpts for review purposes) without the express written permission of Tom Hutchison. All names, characters, events and locales in this publication are entirely fictional. Any resemblance to actual persons (living or dead), events or places, without satiric intent, is coincidental.

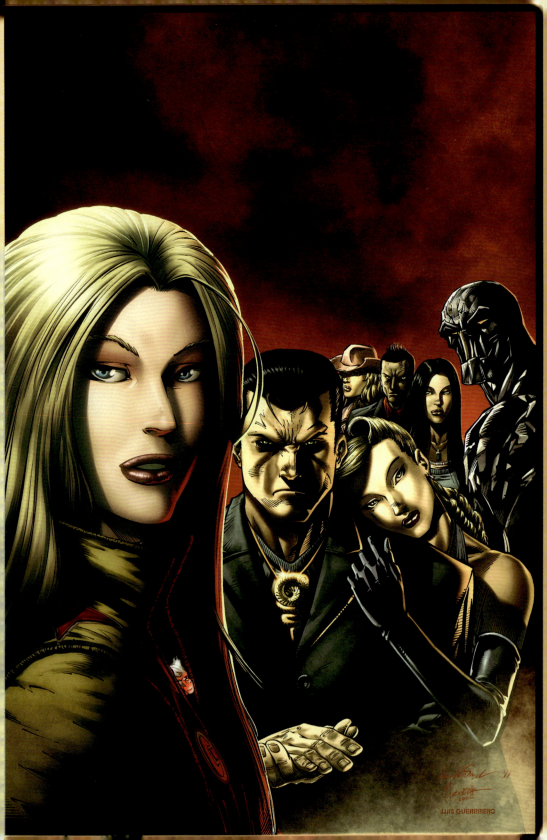

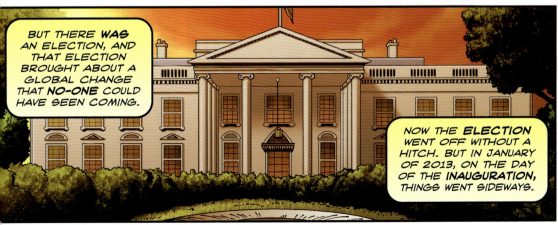

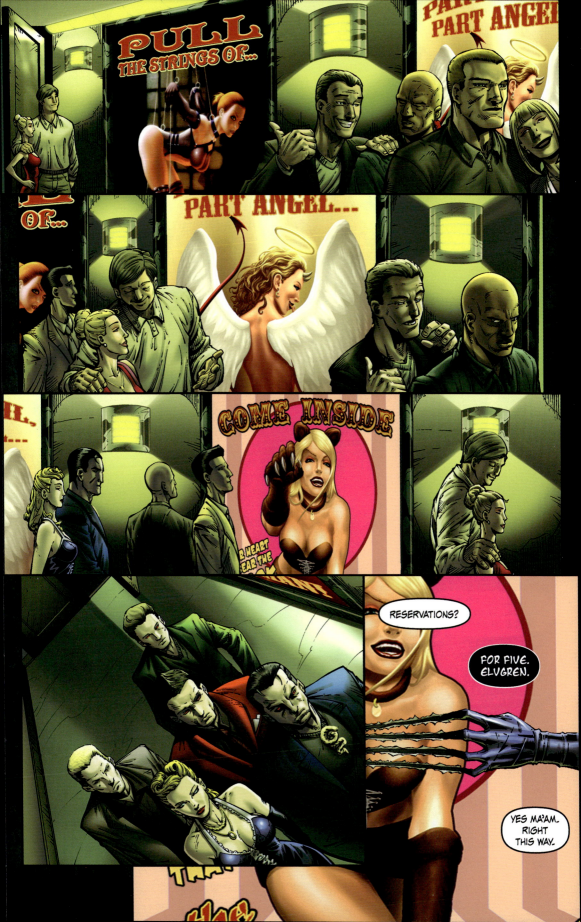

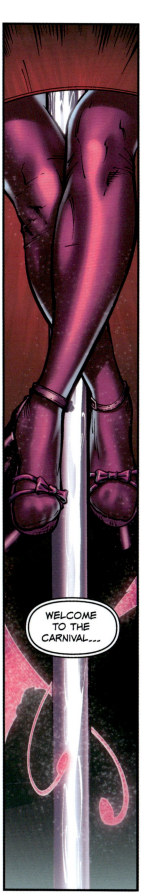

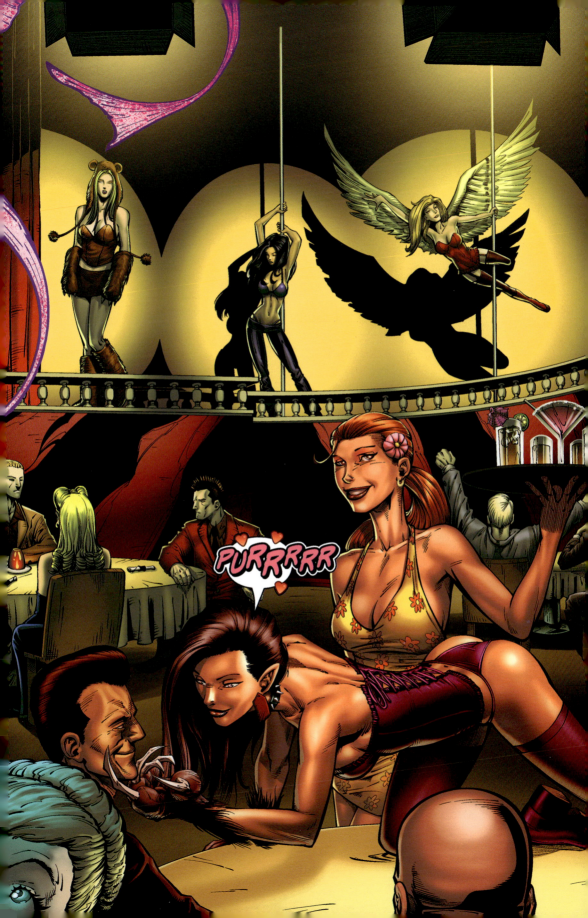

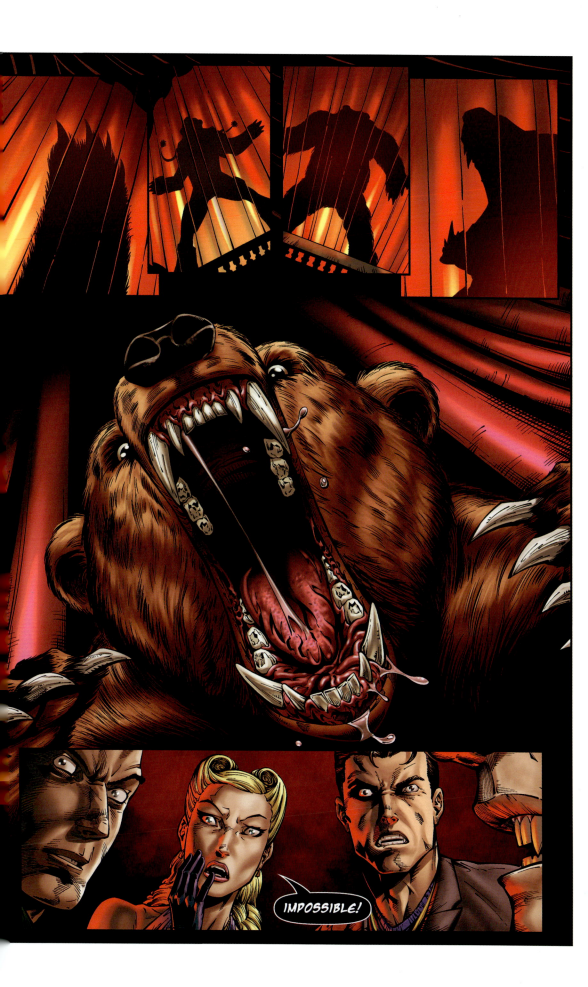

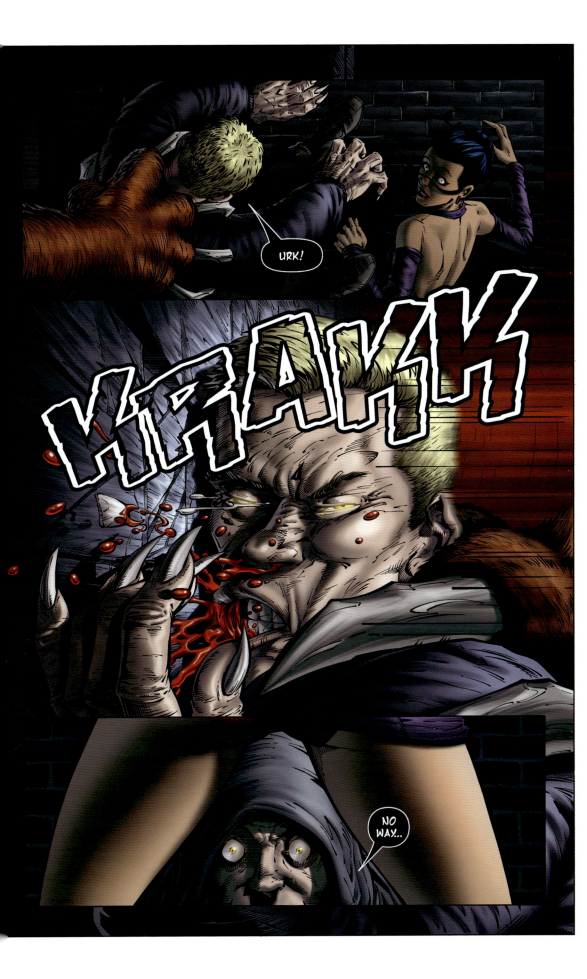

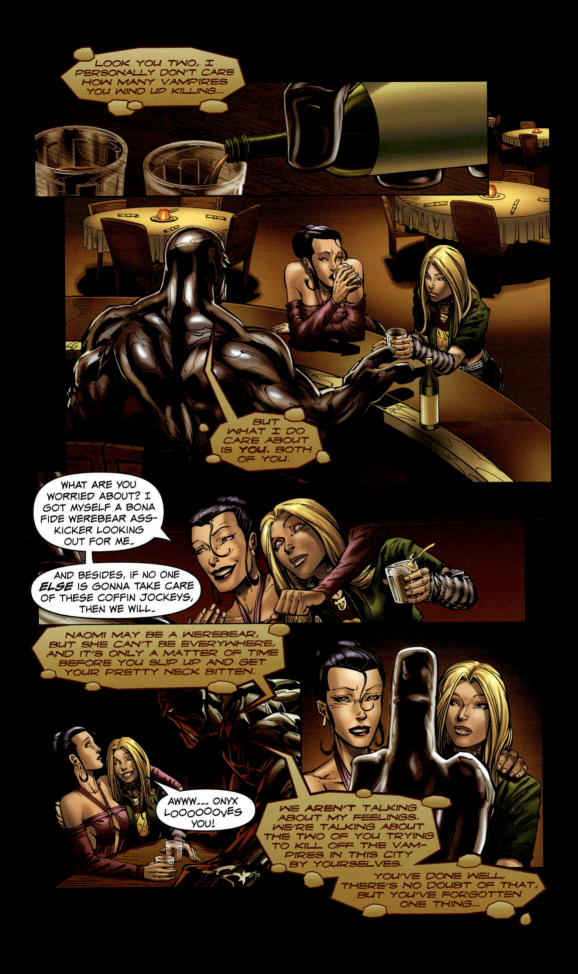

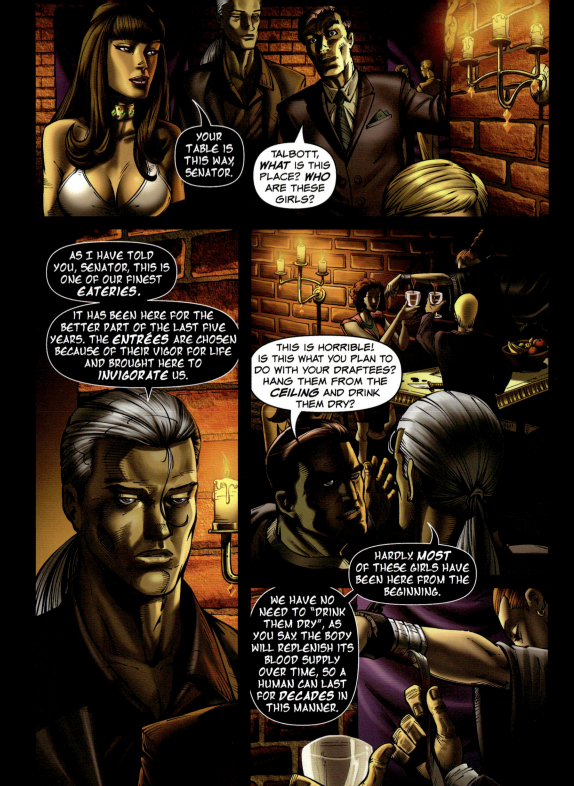

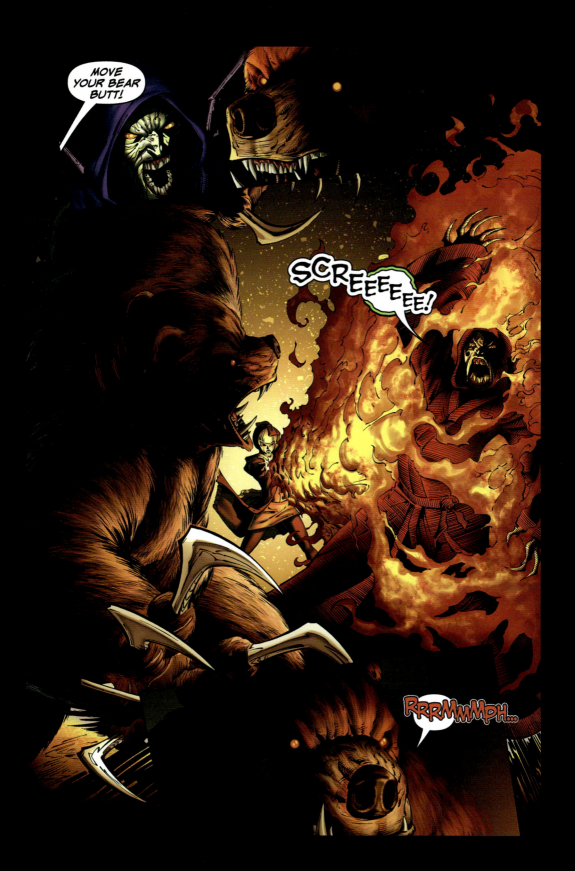

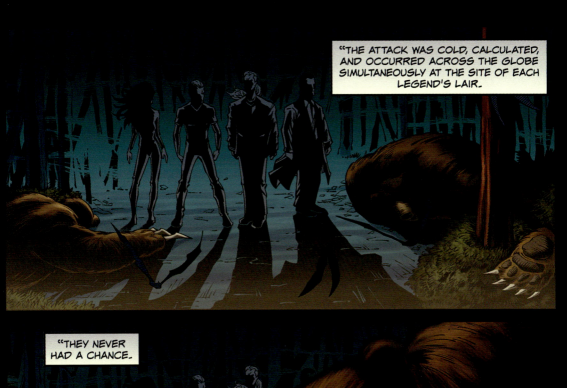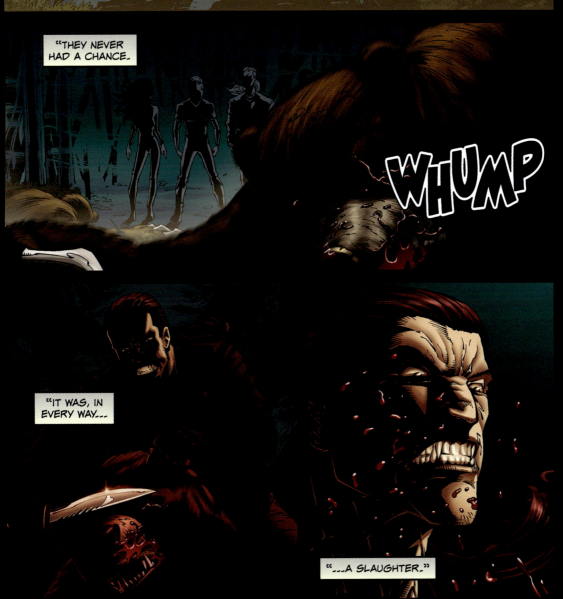

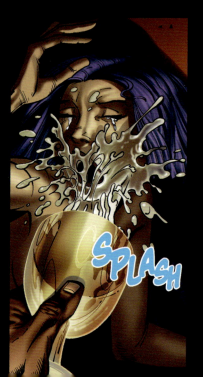

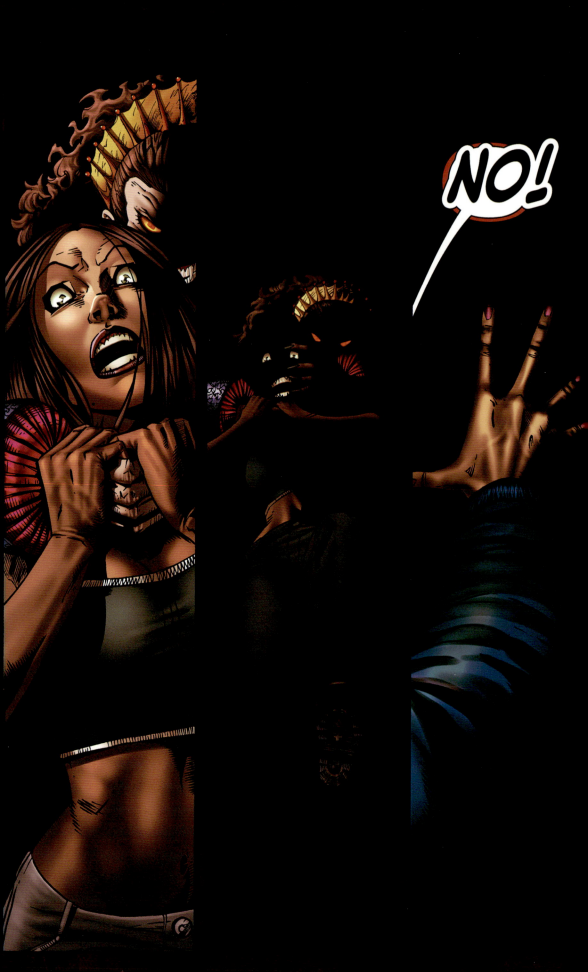

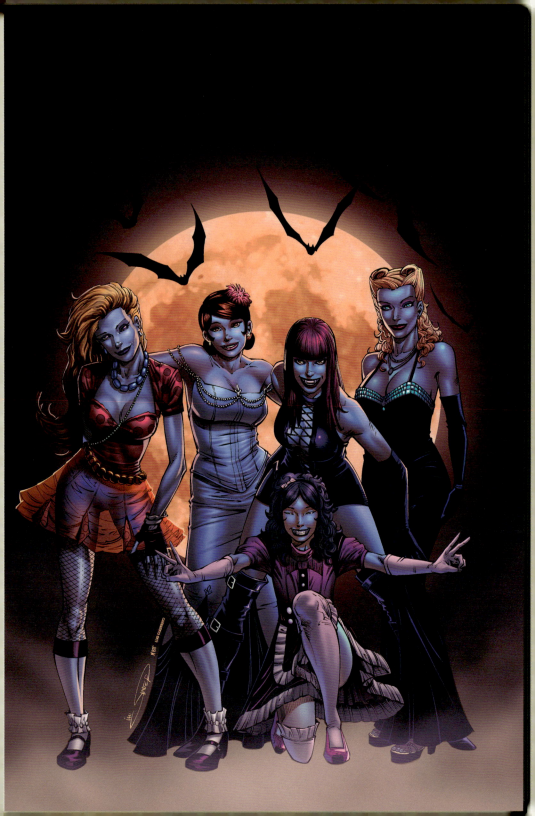

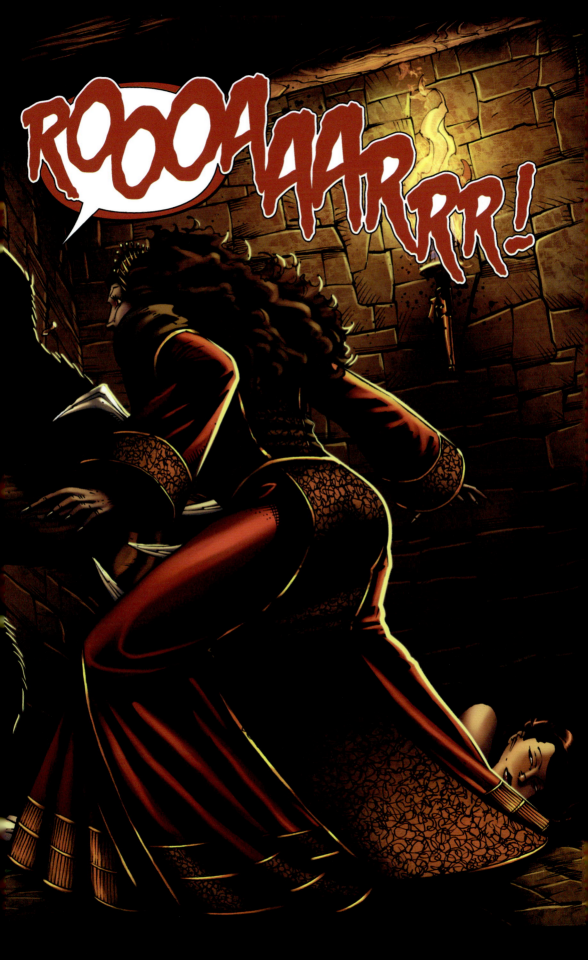

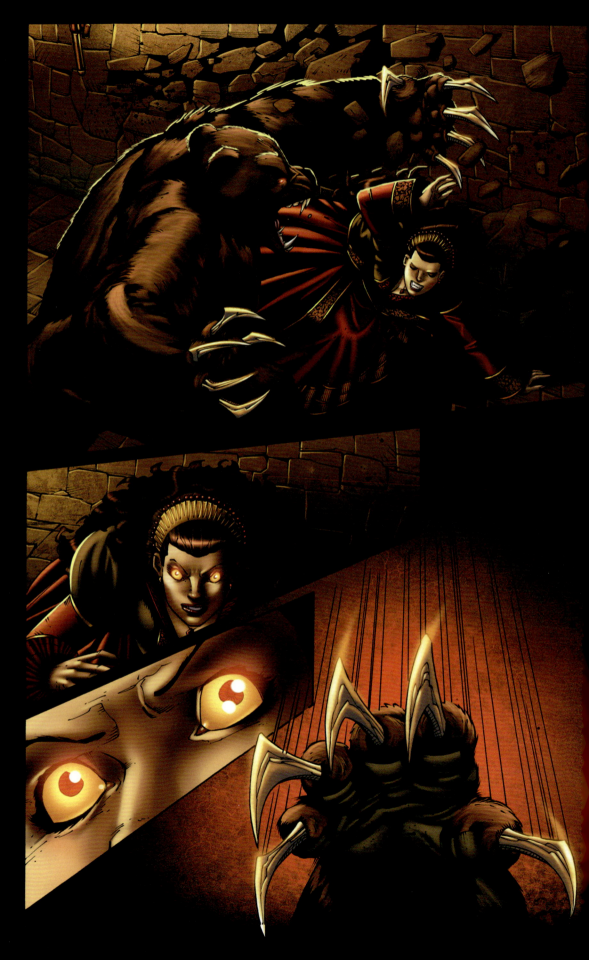

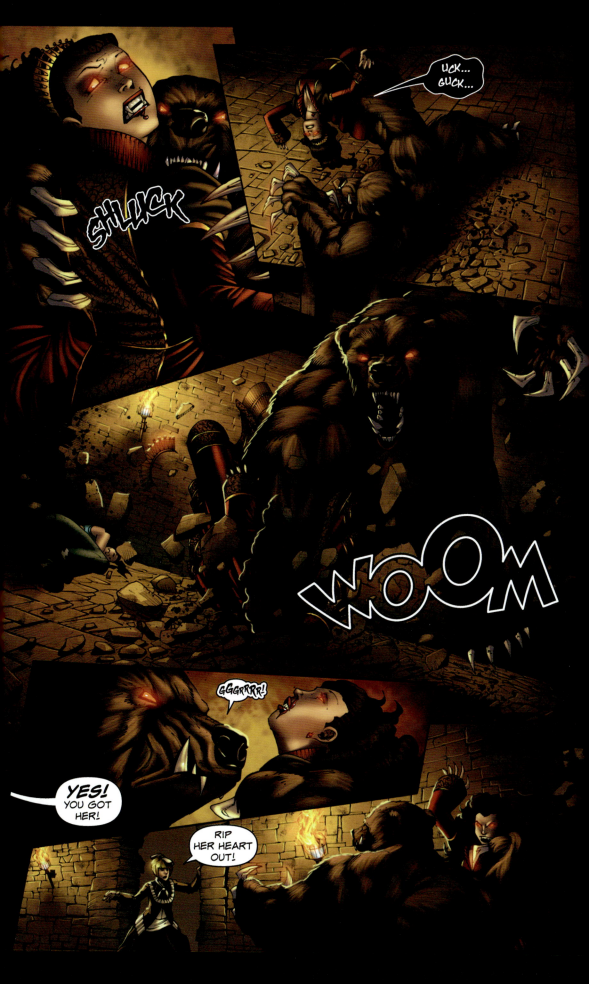

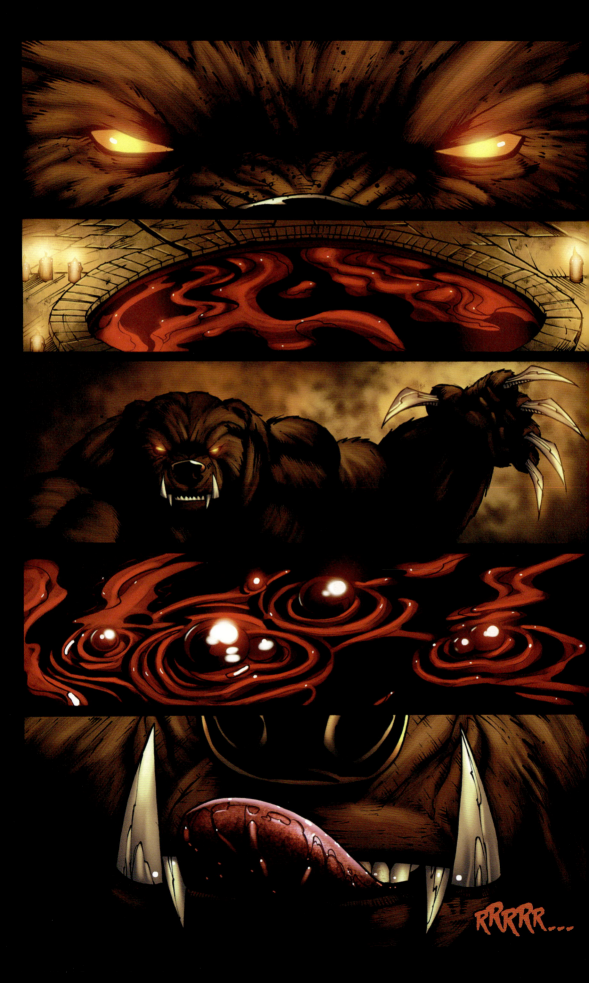

NAOMI IS A MYSTERY TO THE WORLD THAT URSA MINOR TAKES PLACE IN, AND EVEN TO THOSE THAT WORK ON THE BOOK. ONLY WRITER TOM HUTCHISON KNOWS WHO SHE REALLY IS AND WHAT MAKES HER TICK. AS THE NEW ONGOING SERIES STARTS, WE WILL START TO LEARN FAR MORE ABOUT THIS TRAGIC HERO.

NAOMI

DESIGN BY IAN SNYDER

APRIL
DESIGN BY IAN SNYDER

Readers of Ursa Minor took a shine to April pretty much instantly. Her unique clothing sparked a flame in our readers hearts and minds. After all, who doesn't like a girl in combat boots?

JESSE
DESIGN BY IAN SNYDER

Jesse was the bull riding cowgirl who never stood a chance. But even with characters that are destined to die, design is always considered important. Her hot pink riding outfit would have been fun to see in action.

VICTOR

DESIGN BY IAN SNYDER

VICTOR IS THE LEAD LYCANTHROPE TAGGER IN THE UNITED STATES

YAKUZA

DESIGN BY IAN SNYDER

IN JAPAN, THE YAKUZA ARE ALMOST ALL CREATURES OF THE NIGHT... BUT THAT DOESN'T MEAN THEY ARE ALL ONLY VAMPIRES...

LADY BATHORY

DESIGN BY IAN SNYDER

DRACULA AND THE BOYS GET ALL THE PRESS, BUT LADY BATHORY IS AS VICIOUS AND BLOODTHIRSTY AS ANY VAMPIRE. HER LEGEND HAS LIVED FOR CENTURIES, AND NOAMI IS ABOUT TO GET A HISTORY LESSON...UP CLOSE AND PERSONAL.

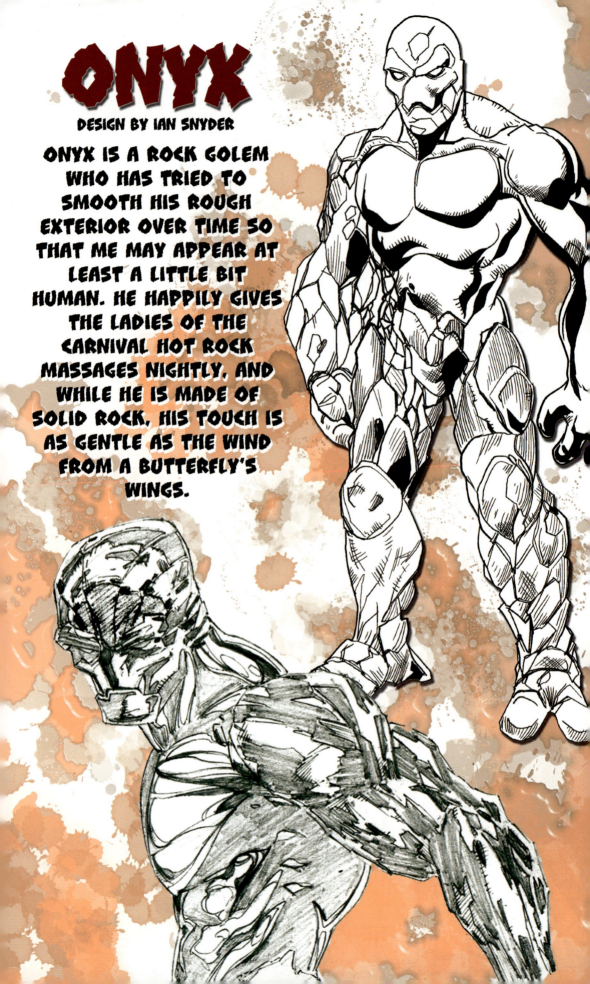

ONYX

DESIGN BY IAN SNYDER

ONYX IS A ROCK GOLEM WHO HAS TRIED TO SMOOTH HIS ROUGH EXTERIOR OVER TIME SO THAT ME MAY APPEAR AT LEAST A LITTLE BIT HUMAN. HE HAPPILY GIVES THE LADIES OF THE CARNIVAL HOT ROCK MASSAGES NIGHTLY, AND WHILE HE IS MADE OF SOLID ROCK, HIS TOUCH IS AS GENTLE AS THE WIND FROM A BUTTERFLY'S WINGS.